WALLOP AND WHIZZ AND THE BOTTLE OF FIZZ

Philip Hawthorn
Illustrated by Kim Blundell
Designed by Non Figg
Edited by Jenny Tyler

This book contains two creatures, who
Are trying hard to hide from you.
There's Fred The Frog, who wears a cloak,
(And loves to croak the latest joke)
And Kate The Cat, who wears a hat,
(For catching rats and things like that).

To make them shake and shout with rage,
Just find them both on every page...

For Silas

Come lightning flash! Come storm-black cloud!
Come thunder crash, (but not too loud),
Transport us back to times long gone,
Before cartoons and CD ROM,
To see two wizards, come draw near!
Meet Whizz and Wallop...ZAP!   Oh dear...

Now this man's called Lord Robbie Duff,
Not really right, but close enough.
He's been the wizards' boss and friend,
Since Lady Flora met her end:
While spotting birds, a giant puffin
Had swooped and munched her like a muffin.

But back to business ~ here we go,
We want two wizards...ZAP!   Oh no...

I don't believe it ~ Dirk and Daisy,
Lord Robbie's kids who drive him crazy.
There's no mean thing they wouldn't try,
To make you cross or scream or cry.
You'd find them both, at any time,
Bombarding pets with gunge and slime.

Last time now, fingers crossed, touch wood.
Let's hope for wizards...ZAP! Oh good.

They're working hard on two new spells,
(Excuse the mess and niffy smells);
They want to win, like each magician,
The annual wizard competition.
They little knew what lay in store;
Far more than what they bargained for...

3

Chapter One: The Wizards concoct their spells...well, almost.

It all began at frantic speed,
The wizards grabbed the things they'd need.
Each one was sure his spell would be,
The winning magic recipe.

"I want," said Whizz, "some cockroach skins,
Two tiny tins of fishes' fins,
Some slimy snails and gerbils' tails,
And thirty dirty fingernails.
The powdered horns of seven sheep,
The breath of someone deep asleep,
A frozen petal from a rose,
Three drops of baby's runny nose.
An eyelash from a big gorilla,
And half a hairy caterpillar,
Some gooey gum, a lizard's tongue,
And plums wrapped up in beetles' dung."

Now Wallop on the other hand,
Had something very different planned.
"You take an ounce of camel's cough,
A mangled moth that's going off,
Around a pound of muddy ground,
A flea that fell in tea and drowned.
Some dandruff and an adder's puff,
A bit of belly button fluff,
A bee's last sneeze, a spider's knees,
And Chinese cheese with pickled peas.
You shake the spell, then gently boil it,
And bake it well in Granny's toilet."

They both then said, "To finish it,
I need a bit of children's spit."
Disaster struck ~ they'd run right out,
But then, without, they heard a shout...

Then having just kicked Grandad's shin,
Both Dirk and Daisy tumbled in.
With mischief eyes they looked to check
For things that they could break or wreck.
"Oh heck!" said Whizz, "That's all we need."
But Wallop smiled, "It is indeed!".

He asked the kids for their consent,
To get that last ingredient.
But being mean, they'd not agree,
To give saliva willingly.
They whined, "Get lost, you weirdy nerds!"
(And other even ruder words.)
Then stuck their tongues out ~ but at this,
Whizz saw a chance they couldn't miss.

They grabbed two sponges, then they flung
Them both at each protruding tongue.
So when, of course, the missiles hit,
They soaked up just a little spit.

6

The wizards then with joyful yells,
Were able to complete their spells.
The lab was cloaked with sparks and smoke;
The children choked, then Wallop spoke,
"Behold! The world's most Fizzy Drink.
It's utter genius, don't you think?
The bubbles range from pink to blue,
(It makes your burps all fizzy, too.)"

But Whizz said, "Though I'm quite impressed,
My Never-Empty Bottle's best.
However many drinks you pour,
You'll find there's always gallons more."
They argued then, with dreadful din,
About which magic spell would win.

The kids, still peeved at being deceived,
Perceived a plan, which then they weaved.
So Daisy chirped, "The answer is,
To use the Bottle for the Fizz."
The wizards stopped, "Combine resources?
Of course! We'll both be *tour de forces*."

7

Contestants came from far and near,
To win "Magician Of The Year",
A week of trauma, strain and tension,
To find the greatest spell invention:

A book whose pages turned themselves,
A shell you used to speak to elves.
A bag of ice that kept you warm,
An instant indoor thunderstorm.
A pen that made your writing neat,
A sweet that tasted just like meat.
Four beetles who had formed a band,
(A world tour was already planned).
A magic rope, some non-slip soap,
A tiny X-ray telescope.
And not forgetting Wend The Witch,
Who'd made a switch that made you twitch.

Then just before they broke for tea,
A wizard said, "Mine's called T.V.
I press this knob, now watch the screen,
And moving pictures will be seen."
The judges frowned and, when he'd gone,
Said, "Can't see that one catching on."

Whizz whispered, "Agh! It's nearly us!"
"I know that," Wallop said, "Don't fuss.
It's all in hand," then added, grinning,
"There's nothing now can stop us winning."

But as he spoke, beneath their seats,
Were Dirk and Daisy, champion cheats.
They shook the wizards' bottle fast,
While giggling, "Ha! Revenge at last!"

The wizards' turn soon came, so Whizz
Picked up the bottle with the Fizz.
Then Wallop cried, "We give to you,
Not one amazing spell ~ but two!"
He popped the top, then gave a shout,
As loads of liquid spurted out.
The bottle rocket zoomed away,
Propelled by jets of fizzy spray.
The wizards held as tight as glue,
With Dirk and Daisy on each shoe.

They sailed through clouds and soared so high,
They thought they'd soon run out of sky.
They flew for hours, then fell at last,
Towards a castle ~ very fast.
But thankfully inside its walls,
Was something soft to break their falls.
"Wherever are we?" Wallop said,
To which a voice boomed, "On my head!"

A huge man stood, "I'm so annoyed,
I think I'll have you all destroyed."
Whizz mumbled, "Oh...well...how d'you do?
I'm Whizz, he's Wallop ~ who are you?"
"King Slaughter's who I am," he roared,
And drew his mean and massive sword.
"I can't stand kids, I loathe all wizards,
I'll cut your throats and slit your gizzards.
I'll slice you all like French salami!"
"Oh yeah," said Daisy, "And whose army?"

The wizards cringed and said, "We're dead."
But no swift sword blow came, instead
They just heard sobbing, lame and limp.
"Good grief!" the kids said, "What a wimp!"

10

Just then a girl came, hopping mad;
She bellowed, "Who's upset my Dad?"
She said her name was Princess Vicious,
   And how, in spite of being ambitious,
They'd never fought in any wars,
      Nor been marauding conquerors.
   "We rule a people called the Twees,
         They don't believe in enemies.
      They're nice and good and sweet and soft."
   "Oh yuck! We'd soon change that," Dirk scoffed.

The king stopped crying straightaway,
"You could? All right, you've got one day.
If you succeed, I'll set you free.
If not, I'll kill you...horribly."

So off they went with Princess Vicious,
To try and make the Twees malicious.
The children's scheme, which seemed quite good
Was: be as nasty as they could.
In Tweeland, though, they found far more,
Than any of them bargained for.

The Twees weren't only nice-as-pie,
But NICE in letters five miles high.
The men were tall, with healthy tans,
And fluffy beards and cardigans.
They'd say, "Good-day!" and "Fare thee well!",
They never burped or made a smell.
Among their kind you'd find no hate,
They called each other "bud" and "mate".

The women all wore pretty dresses,
And smiled like airline stewardesses.
They didn't gossip, smoke or swear,
And never told you what to wear.

They all had perfect girls and boys,
Who never fought or made a noise.
   They'd not come home with dirty clothes,
   Or lie or cheat or pick their nose.
   They went to bed as good as gold,
   Cleaned out their pets without being told.
And every sister and her brother,
Shared all their toys and kissed each other.

The whole place gleamed with cleanliness,
   No grime, graffiti, muck or mess.
   Police, of course, were never needed,
   As laws and rules were always heeded.
   For, after all, you'd get no vandals,
   Where everyone wore socks and sandals.

The twins saw this and thought they'd burst.
"Come on," said Dirk, "Let's do our worst."

They plotted dreadful japes and jokes,
On all these unsuspecting folks,
To get the Twees in such a state,
They'd angrily retaliate.

They set to work without delay:
They knocked on doors and ran away,
Tied rusty pails on horse's tails,
And filled up baths with slugs and snails.
They knocked off hats, made chairs collapse,
Dropped spiders into teachers' laps.
Put fleas in people's nice clean sheets,
And glue on top of toilet seats.
They sprinkled soap flakes like confetti,
On top of pasta and spaghetti.
It was ~ in all the roads and streets,
Like trick or treat, without the treats.

But though the twins were vile and wild,
The Twees just looked, and mildly smiled.

Then Dirk and Daisy, very stressed,
Yelled, "Death to Niceness ~ Bad is best!"
They popped balloons and punctured balls,
Scrawled naughty slogans on the walls,
Beheaded flowers using sticks,
Smashed fences with karate kicks.
Called older people nasty names,
Broke children's toys and spoiled their games,
And other things best left unsaid,
Involving wasps and chocolate spread.

The princess laughed, "What great ideas,
I've not had so much fun in years."
The wizards groaned with heads in hands,
"The horrid little hooligans."
But then they saw a group of Twees,
Approaching, slowly, on their knees.

The Princess cheered, "What's this I see?"
And Daisy shouted, "Victory!"
"We're saved," said Dirk, "How satisfying.
They're creeping, crawling ~ and they're crying!"

Alas, poor twins, when they got near,
The truth became completely clear.
The Twees were weeping, not with grief,
But joy and bliss beyond belief.

Their leader, then, with weedy voice,
Said, "Twuly do our hearts wejoice!"
The Twees behind him all agreed,
"Wejoice!" they simpered, "Yes, indeed!"

The leader grinned, "We give you thanks,
For all your weally twiffic pwanks,
We laughed so much we nearly died!"
"Ooh, weally, yes!" the others cried.
"To show our gweat appweciation,
Do please accept this invitation.
It's to a banquet, which will be
Inside a gween and gwand marquee.
Tonight's a night to celebwate,
We'll eat and dwink and stay up late!"
The others chorused, "Ooh, how gweat!
No bed for us till ten past eight."

The Twees then left. Whizz sighed, "Ah, food!
My tummy moans in gratitude."
"Oh, don't be silly," Daisy said,
"No point being grateful when you're dead."
The Princess drew her sword, "Well, quite.
My dad'll keep his threat, all right.
Unless you make the Twees rebel,
You'll end up in his torture cell."

Chapter Three: Inside the marquee, in need of a pretty good plan...

The marquee buzzed with busy Twees,
Preparing the festivities.
The tent effused pale pinks and blues
(Though not, of course, in shades you'd choose),
With fiddly bows and fancy frills,
And napkins shaped like daffodils.

The food they ate was quite divine,
With fine non-alcoholic wine.
The Chief Twee rose, "Now as the host,
I weally must pwopose a toast."
Then 'Ping!' at once the wizards knew
Exactly what they had to do.
Whizz stood, "Before your speech, Oh Chief,
May *I* speak? I'll be very brief:

"To be your special guests, we're blessed.
I now express this one request:
That for the toast we give to you,
A drink to clink our glasses to."
Then Wallop poured each Twee some Fizz,
And Whizz said, "Now then, *my* toast is...
To our new friendship, if you please!"
"Our Fwiendship!" echoed all the Twees.

When everybody's drink was slurped,
The Chief Twee stood and ...RURRRGHGH! He burped.
The Twees just stared, but then the spell
Made *them* begin to burp as well.
Though shocked, it wasn't long before
With wicked grins they shouted, "More!"
And then they started throwing food,
And singing, "Oooh! We're weally wude!"

Then Whizz explained, "The Fizz just gave
The Twees the chance to misbehave!"
The princess smiled at all the mess,
As Twees threw custard at her dress.
Meanwhile amidst the raucous riot,
The twins just stood there, strangely quiet.

With all this windy burping in it,
The tent grew bigger by the minute.
Just like a great hot-air balloon,
Which then took off towards the moon.
The kids, the wizards, princess too,
All grabbed a rope and up they flew.
Past trees and clouds and birds they rose,
And startled starlings, baffled crows.
Then after several hours of flight,
They sighed as home came into sight.

They bumped to earth with great precision,
Back at the magic competition,
Just as, it being the final day,
The prizes lunch was underway.
Then Whizz said, "Hi! We're back ~ don't worry.
Now what's to eat? Mmm ~ chicken curry."

Lord Robbie (who, in case you're hazy,
Is Dad to dreadful Dirk and Daisy),
Looked lovingly ~ not at his kids,
But at the woman in their midst:
The princess. It was plain to see,
They'd both been smitten instantly.
He knelt on one knee to exclaim,
"Please marry me...um...what's your name?"
The princess blushed suspiciously,
And answered, "Princess Vish...er...Twee."

Then, more amazing, both his twins,
As good as gold, with saintly grins,
Danced round and round and sweetly cried,
"Thwee cheers for Daddy and his bwide!"
(They'd learned being kind is quite OK ~
Things can't get better, can they, eh?)

Well yes ~ the judges stopped their dinners,
And said, "Whizz, Wallop you're the winners.
Your magic Fizz is best ~ it's clear
You're both Magicians Of The Year!"
And then the great assembled throng,
Erupted into joyful song.

So everything seems cut and dried,
And all loose endings neatly tied.
A sunset finish, joy and laughter,
And all lived happy ever after.
But this is just page twenty-one,
There's three more pages yet to come...

The wedding and the grand reception,
Were loved by all without exception.
(For foreign guests, the buffet sandwiches,
Had labels in a dozen languages).

But then there came a fearsome bellow,
To chill your blood, and make it yellow,
And everyone was quickly seized
By hordes of mean and nasty Twees,
(Who, having now turned bad, were willing
To have a go at wars and killing).

King Slaughter then rode in, sword drawn,
And boomed, "You'll wish you'd not been born!
We'll pillage all your village, then,
    We'll slay and slaughter all the men.
    We'll kill the girls and kiss the goats ~
    Err, no...I'll just consult my notes...
That's...kill the goats and kiss the girls,
    And plunder jewels, gold and pearls.
    And do whatever things we please!"
"Oh, yes indeed!" growled all the Twees.

Lord Robbie spoke, "Your majesty,
It doesn't seem quite fair to me,
To threaten to invade our nation,
Without a hint of explanation."

The King looked round, "Hmmm...well, for one,
We love this job, it's really fun.
The other reason," sighed King Slaughter,
"Is in remembrance of my daughter.
A week ago she disappeared,
In circumstances highly weird."
He then roared, "Agh! That's not the point ~
My sword is! Ha! Let's wreck the joint!"

The Twees yelled, "Death!"...But suddenly...

...A voice cried, "Father, look ~ it's me!"

The princess stood, pure beauty's dream,
More lovely than a huge ice cream.
King Slaughter stared, his eyes all dewy,
The Twees said, "Oooo!" and went all gooey.
The Princess smiled, "Dad, be a peach,
And come and do your wedding speech."

The celebrations then resumed,
And love between the nations bloomed.
But what of Wallop? What of Whizz?
They'd sneaked outside to hide the Fizz,
In case its magic froth and bubble,
Caused anybody further trouble.
They did, however, just decide
To have a swig for groom and bride...

The fireworks, later, thrilled each guest,
But all agreed on which were best:
The spangly, sparkling whizzy blizzards,
Of two extremely Fizzy Wizards.

First published in 1996 by Usborne Publishing Ltd, Usborne House, 83-85 Saffron Hill, London EC1N 8RT, England. Text copyright © 1996 Philip Hawthorn.
Pictures copyright © 1996 Usborne Publishing Ltd. The name Usborne and the device ♛ are Trade Marks of Usborne Publishing Ltd. All rights reserved. No part
of this publication may be reproduced, stored in a retrieval system or transmitted by any form or by any means, electronic, mechanical, photocopy, recording or
otherwise, without the prior permission of the publisher. First published in America in August 1996. Universal edition. Printed in Portugal.